Published in the United States by Random House Children's Books, a division of Random
House, Inc., New York. Originally published in Australia as *The Wrong Thing* by Viking,
an imprint of Penguin Books Australia, Camberwell, in 2006.

RANDOM HOUSE and colophon are registered trademarks of Random House, Inc.

www.randomhouse.com/kids
Educators and librarians, for a variety of teaching tools, visit us at
www.randomhouse.com/teachers

Library of Congress Cataloging-in-Publication Data
Carmody, Isobelle.
[Wrong thing]
Magic night / Isobelle Carmody ; illustrated by Declan Lee. — 1st American ed.
p. cm.
Originally published under title: The wrong thing.
SUMMARY: Late one night a strange, flittery skittery thing enters the house on a big gust
of wind and, although only Hurricane the cat sees it, it leaves enchantment in its wake.
ISBN 978-0-375-83918-4 (trade) — ISBN 978-0-375-93918-1 (lib. bdg.)
[1. Cats—Fiction. 2. Fairies—Fiction. 3. Magic—Fiction.] I. Lee, Declan, ill. II. Title.
PZ7.C2176Mag 2007
[E]—dc22
2006025439

PRINTED IN CHINA
10 9 8 7 6 5 4 3 2 1

First American Edition

Magic Night

ISOBELLE CARMODY

ILLUSTRATED BY DECLAN LEE

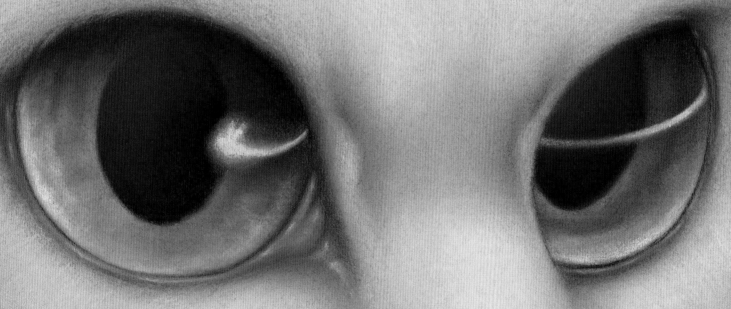

Random House 🏠 New York

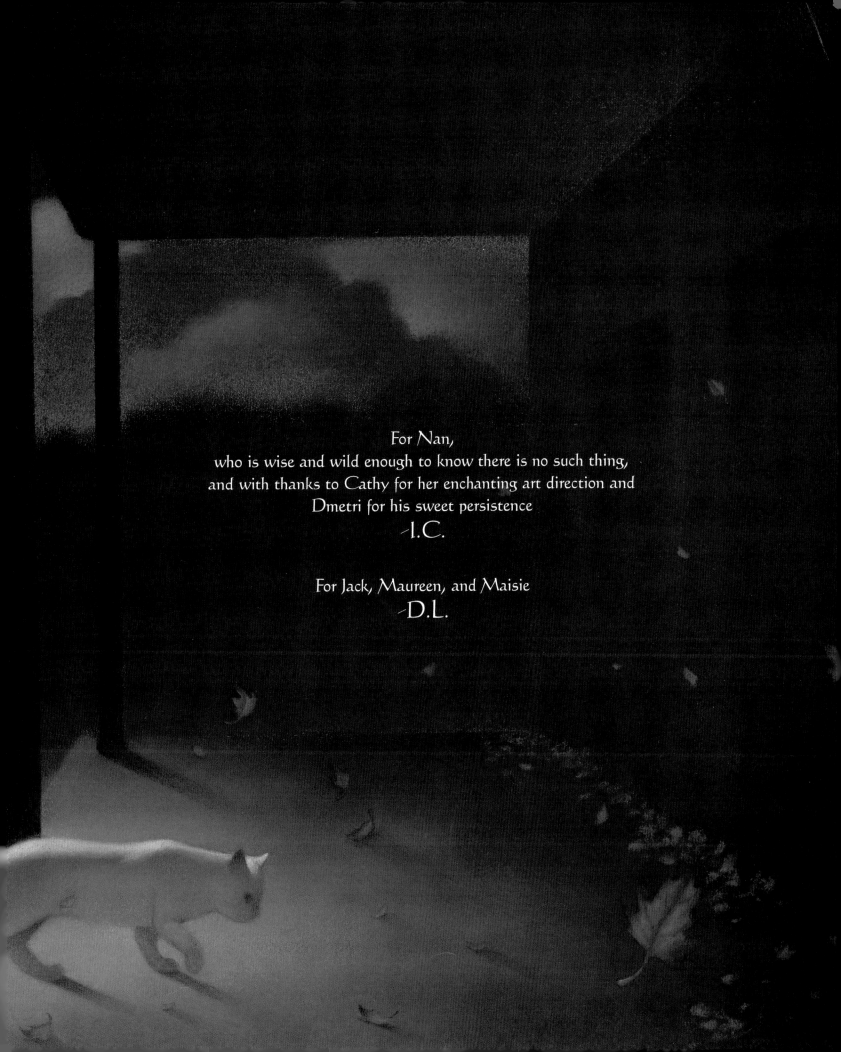

For Nan,
who is wise and wild enough to know there is no such thing,
and with thanks to Cathy for her enchanting art direction and
Dmetri for his sweet persistence
—I.C.

For Jack, Maureen, and Maisie
—D.L.

Hurricane the cat comes in with a great gust of wind.

Something flies past his ear. Is it a moth? Is it a firefly?

Hurricane sniffs, but he does not know this smell.

Something strange has gotten into his house

and things are beginning to change.

Hurricane does not like change!

The strangeness makes his ears itch
and his fur stand on end.

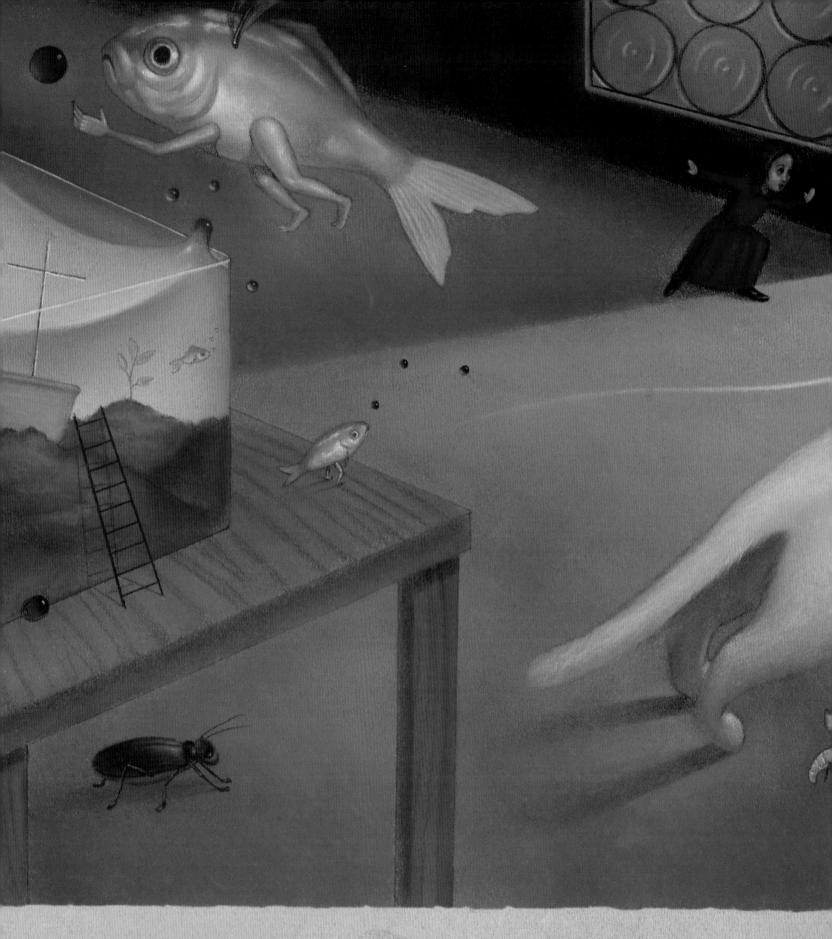

Hurricane must protect his family
from this flittery, skittery thing.

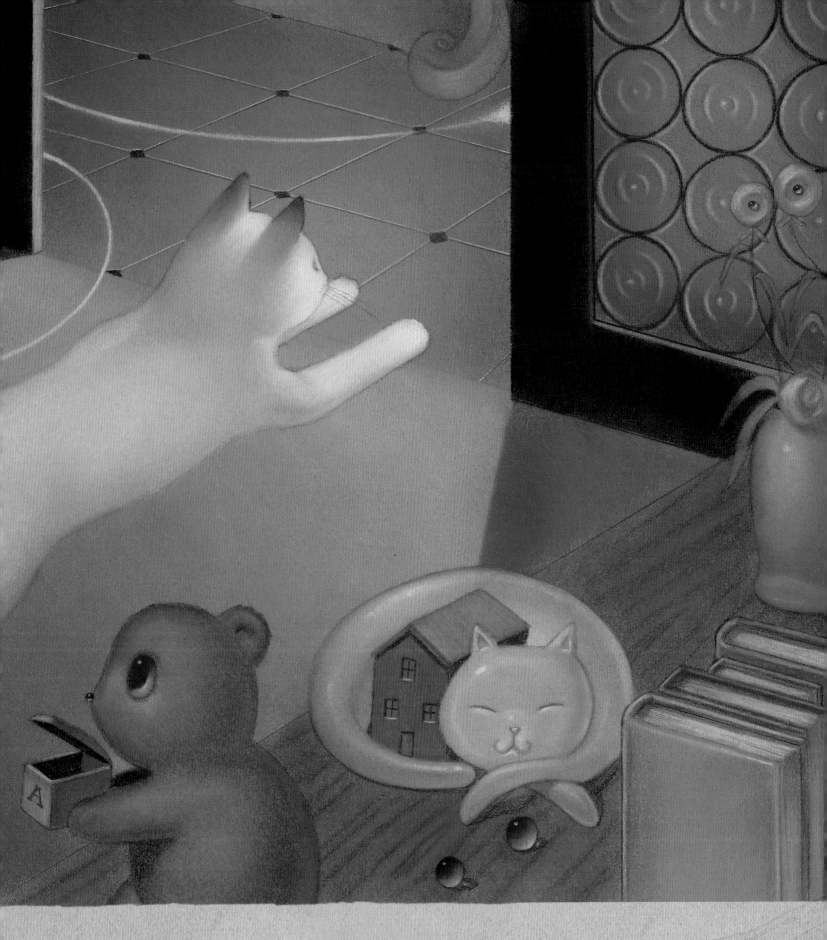

He pounces.

He has it between his paws. It is soft!

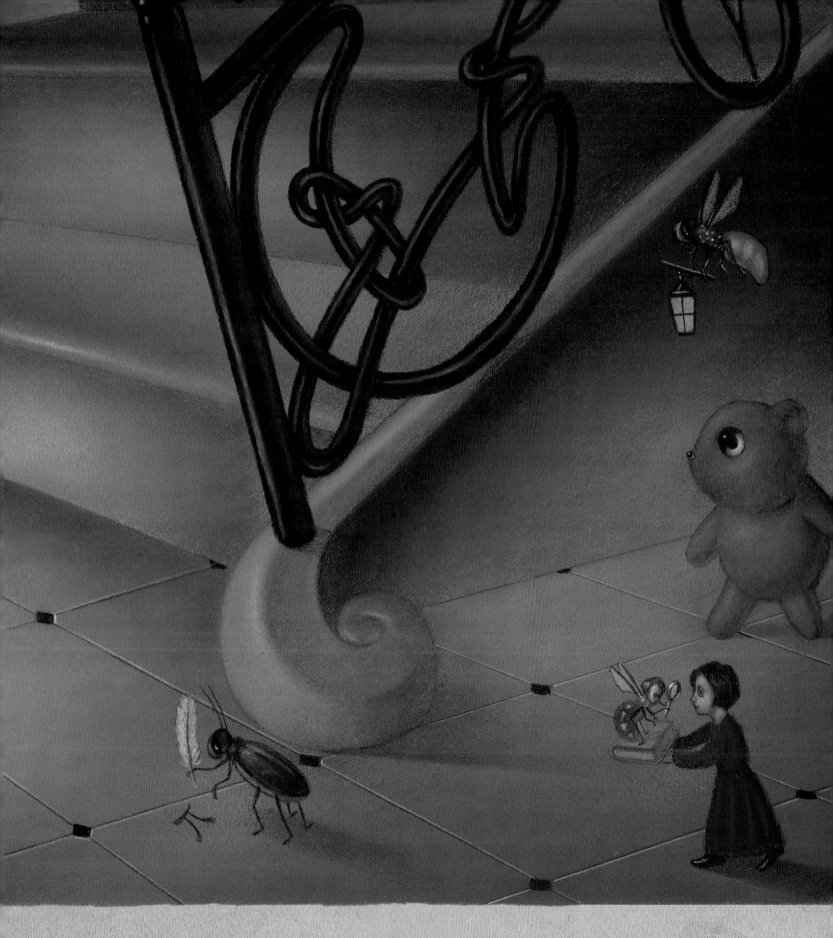

He touches it with his tongue. It is sweet!

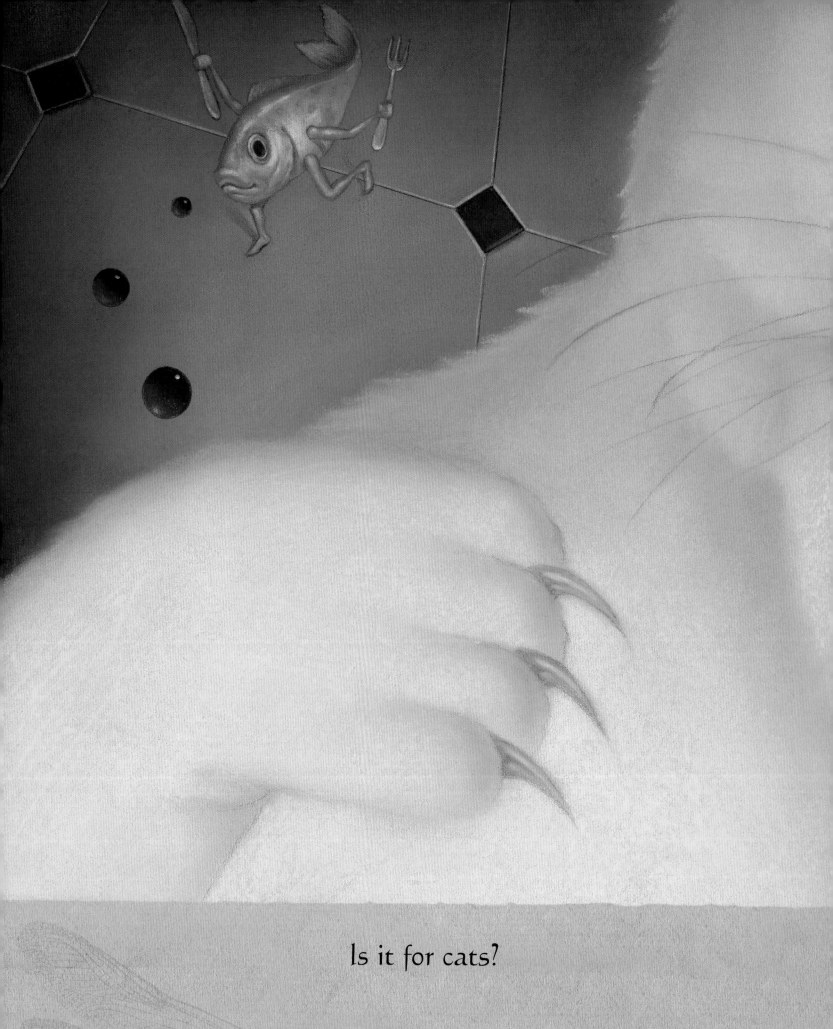

Is it for cats?

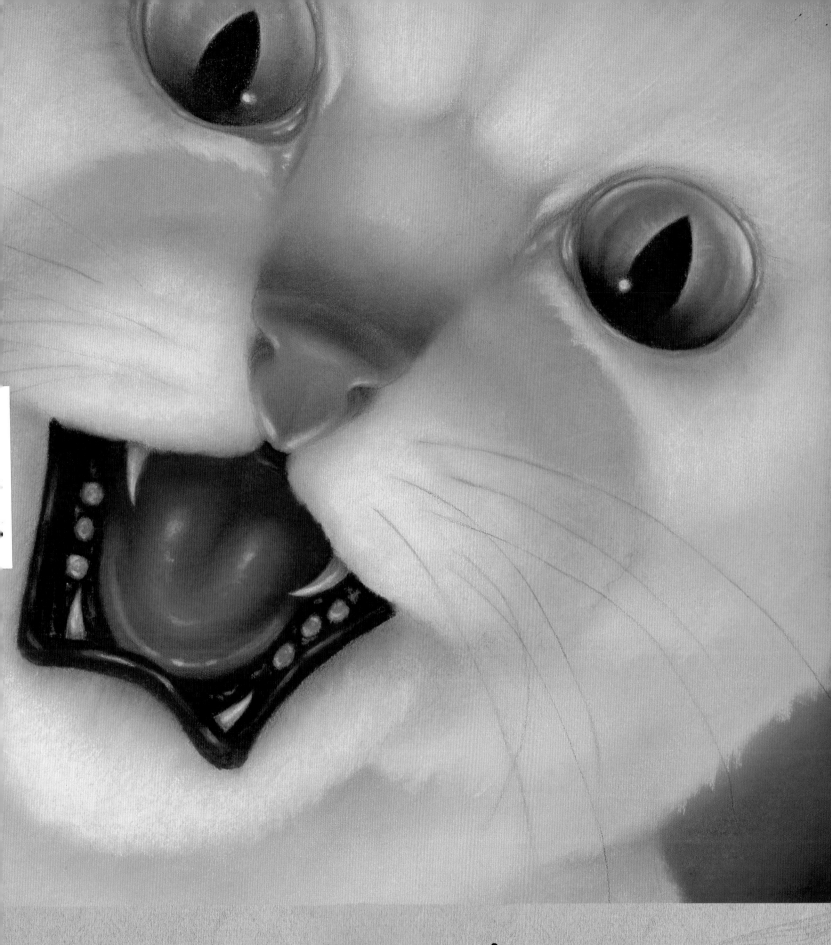

Is it for eating?

No!

This strange thing is a strong thing!

Hurricane could make his people wake and look,
but would they see?

This is a house where everything has its place
and every place has its thing.

There is no place for this strange thing.

What does it want here?

What does it bring?

Hurricane wonders.

It comes to the baby. It stares and stares.

Then Hurricane sees—and understands!
This strange thing is a young thing.

This strange thing is a *lost* thing!
It belongs some otherwhere.

Hurricane pushes the window open to let it fly out.

It flits across the road to the shore to where a ship waits.

I found the strangest place,
it tells its mama, who laughs.

Hurricane watches them sail away and hopes
the strange thing will return some magic night.